CW00808336

Hayly Stems
The Tide

Written By

Elizabeth Thompson

Illustrations By

Gaurav Bhatnagar

This book belongs to

_____

ISBN: 9798985452600 (Paperback)
ISBN: 9798985452617 (Hardback)

Library of Congress Control No. 2022903288

Any references to historical events, real people or real places are used fictitiously. Names, characters, and places are products of the author's imagination.

Cover and Illustrations by: Gaurav Bhatnagar
Edited by: Lor Bingham

Publisher: Elizabeth Thompson
             Coral Springs, Florida, 33065
Website: www.akosuamaatcreative.com

- <u>Dedication</u> -

This book is dedicated to my four sons, my loves:
Dafidi,
O. Morenikeji,
Hayley
and Seth.

As children I protected you from the very start, held you so tightly and fondly, struggling oftentimes to create space to reflect on the gift of your presence amid the chaos. Words can not describe how proud I am of the men you all are and have become.

You are the four stars in my night sky who always shine brightly, illuminating my path, keeping me honest, encouraging me motivating me to be better than the day before.

I am in awe of you, thankful to the Universe for allowing me to guide you.

I love you now and always.
Mommy,
Elizabeth

Parent Note:

Thank you to all of you, especially the parents who have purchased this book.

I created this work to offer youngsters a voice, to create a space for them. For those who have had their innocence taken away from them, for those who have survived their childhoods despite being neglected and/or abused by adults who should have loved and cherished them.

While the characters and tale are fictitious, the challenges presented are all too true and real for far too many of our young girls and boys. Sadly, too many of us adults can recall an improper remark or inappropriate touch as children that we should never have been exposed to. Too many of us see the thieves of our innocence living amongst us as though their actions did not matter.

I hope that this book encourages youngsters and adults to be courageous and daring.

I hope it encourages a youngster to speak up if he or she has been molested, verbally abused, or physically assaulted by anyone, especially a family member.

Dear Parents,

I hope that when they tell us
We pay attention and really listen.

I hope that when they tell us
We hug and hold them tight

I hope that when they tell us
We validate them.

I hope that when they tell us
We believe them, and act swiftly in their best interests,

and more than anything

I hope that when they tell us
We love them even more

To the Children:

If an adult has frightened you, hurt you,

Or made you feel alone,

Or made you feel so badly that you wished you'd turned to stone

Tell a person you can trust and please do it right away.

like Hayly did for her best friend Cree,

to keep the Tide at bay.

www.akosuamaatcreative.com

"Healing begins and ends with you."

To Michelle Edwards,
My friend.

Thank you for creating space, for always reminding me that it is when we find the courage to use our voices that our healing begins.

It was a quiet warm Saturday morning as the sun rose over the seaside town of Mount Vernon. 11 yr old Hayly Simmons awoke to the sound of her Uncle Warren Tide's voice bellowing from the kitchen downstairs. He always bellowed when he spoke, Hayly was not sure why. Uncle Warren's voice was deep, pleasant, melodic, and vibrated throughout their entire house. Hayly smiled, comforted by the sound of her uncle's voice. If Uncle Warren was here, it meant that it really was the weekend. Uncle Warren must have come to bring Mom and Dad a kit of fish, fruit, and vegetables as he often did on the weekends. She could hear him moving about in the kitchen as she removed the pillow from her head and rolled over. One of her teddy bears fell onto the hardwood floor. She picked it up and was rubbing her eyes when Cocoa, their cocker spaniel, nudged her. He was wagging his tail excitedly and barking.

Hayly sat up in bed, stretched, and took in the beauty of the Mount Vernon sunrise. What a view, she thought. Cocoa barked, looked at Hayly then raced down the stairs. Hayly jumped out of her bed, chased

after him and ended up at the bottom of the stairs near the kitchen dressed in her pajamas. As she approached, she could overhear part of a conversation. "Laban...I miss them, I'll speak to the bishop, see if he can sort things out." Hayly wondered what or who Uncle Warren was talking about.

"Those church folks are understanding, I know them and…… ," Hayly's mom was rummaging around in the fridge and her dad was sitting at the table facing Uncle Warren. Hayly's dad and Uncle Warren each had a mug in their hands. "Good morning, Mom, Dad, Uncle Warren. Dad…?" Hayly said interrupting Uncle Warren. Before she could finish her question Uncle Warren said, ".... can't you see that grown folks are talking?! You know in my day children were seen and not heard Hayly," Uncle Warren continued. The tears welled up in Hayly's eyes as she looked at both her parents and Uncle Warren. "If you want something to cry for, I can give you something to cry for" he continued. Hayly quickly apologized, grabbed Cocoa, and ran to her room. She wiped her eyes, quickly made her bed, showered, and dressed. On her way to her brothers' room, she heard her dad say something to Uncle Warren that Hayly could not hear or understand. "Laban, you had better get that child in hand, she's getting too fresh," said Uncle Warren. Hayly felt bad about interrupting her uncle, she knew he was particularly important so the conversation must have been serious.

Whenever Uncle Warren came to visit, he stayed a while, and her parents made a fuss over him. He was a deacon at Cambridge Baptist church and worked in the churchyard. Everyone liked him and said how hard-working he was, especially Ms. Enid the nosey neighbor... Ms. Enid didn't miss a thing!

Hayly's brothers played with her and Cocoa for a while in their room. Like Hayly's, their window overlooked the seashore, Hayly could see the seagulls diving into the sea looking for a meal. There were children in the water having a fun time playing with a beach ball.

Hayly got ready to go to see her aunt Nina Akosua at the bookstore and coffee shop, the EBB & Flow with her best friend, Cree who usually

joined her. They would have to pass Ms. Enid's house on the way and as usual, Ms. Enid would ask them where they were going, she always liked to know what was happening!

Hayly's family life was quite simple, yet exciting. Cree, Hayly, and her brothers Sean and Richard went to the J. Baldwin Preparatory school on weekdays and took part in many after-school activities. Sadly, Laban and Lisa worked long hours at the local hotel, often leaving them on their own, but they were responsible children, so their parents didn't worry too much. They attended the local church at the weekend, along with Uncle Warren. Everyone in the family attended except Auntie Nina Akosua. Hayly knew that the Ebb & Flow was busy, so her Auntie needed to be there. There were poetry readings and free events for kids there on Sundays; Auntie Nina Akosua always encouraged them to look for the light within themselves more so than in a building.

While Hayly loved her family, she had a soft spot for Auntie Nina Akosua. She was lovely, regal, and welcoming with a presence that was commanding. Auntie Nina Akosua's eyes were mahogany brown which complimented her mocha skin and jet-black hair. Nina Akosua was Lisa Simmons' sister and about 10 years younger, but she seemed so wise well beyond her years, as though she had lived through several lifetimes. When she visited Hayly's house on Friday evenings on her way home from the bookstore Auntie Nina Akosua's energy lit up each and every room. She would bring Hayly essential oils, shea butter, and pretty accessories for her hair. She brought books about Francois-Dominique Toussaint Louverture and the Haitian Revolution, or books by Toni Morrison, Nikki Giovanni, and James Baldwin for Hayly and her brothers to read. Sometimes, she would include something delicious that she had baked at the coffee shop.

Auntie Nina Akosua loved to tell Hayly and her nephews stories about their rich history and recount stories passed down to her about their great grandparents, and other ancestors who lived in West Africa and the diaspora before and after slavery interrupted and disrupted their lives.

Hayly and Cree visited Auntie Nina Akosua at the Ebb &Flow every weekend. Hayly's parents encouraged her to go but Hayly didn't ever need encouragement, she loved visiting her! The girls had fun in her bookshop, and she always treated them to some lunch. They also loved to play with seven-year-old Ashton, Auntie Nina Akosua's son. Hayly asked her Auntie why she wasn't allowed to come around as often as Uncle Warren. She explained that it's because she has a son, and she wasn't married when he was born. Hayly thought that that was very unfair!

The next day they went to church and Hayly felt proud of her uncle's role there, everyone welcomed him. She beamed with pride but wished her Auntie could be there too. Uncle Warren proudly assisted the bishop with his pastoral duties, greeting visitors and members. Church was followed by Sunday dinner with Hayly's family Cree and her mother Tessa. Uncle Warren didn't come.

When they went to school on Monday morning, Hayly shared with her brothers what she had discussed with Auntie Nina. Hayly and Cree had just walked past Uncle Warren when Richard whispered. "Hey Hayly," "you do know that Uncle Warren has his own kids, right? And he is not married to their mom either? Yup? Two teen girls who live with their mom up north." "What?" Hayly exclaimed, shocked. "Yep! But he doesn't see them, I don't know why, but he never married their mother." Hayly couldn't believe that Uncle Warren had children but wasn't married and is still treated in a wonderful way whilst Auntie Nina Akosua wasn't! It just didn't make any sense and it was so unfair!

The days and weeks seemed to fly by. Mondays turned into Tuesdays, Wednesdays came and went and soon Friday and the weekends were there again. Every morning on the way to school Hayly, Cree, Sean, and Richard walked through the churchyard, and they would see Uncle Warren. This morning while her brothers waved gleefully at Uncle Warren as they hurried along Hayly gave him a slightly smaller smile, it was strange thinking he had a secret. She remembered the conversation she had overheard. Maybe his girls were the ones he was talking about, the ones who he said he missed. She began to feel sorry for him, he had looked quite sad at the table. Hayly noticed Uncle Warren speaking to Cree, she wondered what it was about, it was her birthday soon, so maybe it was a surprise about that! She hoped so!

The following weekend, Uncle Warren's voice did not wake her up. She wondered why he hadn't come yet. Maybe he was busy at the church. After she got up, dressed, and played with Cocoa, she went to Cree's house for their usual Saturday outing to see Auntie Nina Akosua. "Good morning Ms. Tessa, how're you," Hayly asked, as she put her bike down in front of Cree's yard and greeted Cree's Mom with a hug.

"I'm good love, "said Tessa. "Gotta go tho. There's food in the kitchen and Cree is still in her room asleep I think. "Bye Cree" Tessa grabbed a bagel, her keys, handbag, and cell phone, opened the screen door, and left.

Cree's home was Hayly's second home, so she knew her way around. It was slightly smaller than Hayly's home, but it was warm. Hayly loved how every room was painted a different color. Hayly peered outside to check on her bike, locked the screened door, then turned and headed to Cree's room. She peeked in the kitchen and saw that breakfast was still on the table. Scrambled eggs, turkey bacon, and pancakes. Yummy, pancakes were Cree and Hayly's favorite. "Cree," Hayly called out, "I'm here." Hayly walked toward Cree's bedroom. The door was closed. Cree's room was just across the hallway from her mother's. "I'm in the restroom Hayly," said Cree. "Oh, ok, I thought you'd gone ahead without me." Hayly joked. "Nah, just don't feel too good this morning," Cree said. Hayly frowned. She hoped it was nothing serious. "Oh no sorry Cree, do you need me to get something for you?" Cree did not reply. Moments later, "Hey Hayly, come here please", asked Cree. Hayly walked toward the bathroom door just as she heard the water running in the sink. "What's up," Hayly asked standing outside the bathroom door. Cree opened the door and dried her hands. Hayly looked at Cree inquisitively. Cree was visibly upset. "Hayly, I have something to ask you. She paused. "Do I smell bad; you know like body odor kinda thing" asked Cree putting her nose toward her underarms. "Smell bad! What? No silly! Why?" Hayly exclaimed. Cree walked toward the kitchen. "Your uncle Warren told me that I smell," Cree said sadly. "What?!!! Uncle Warren? How would he know? When did he say that? " Hayly said, in disbelief. "Shhhh," Cree said. "Why am I shushing Cree, it's just you and me here. Your mom went to work." "Walls have ears," said Cree "Ms. Enid is so nosey." "Cree I don't get it. Why would Uncle Warren say that?" Hayly was confused and hurt by Cree's accusation, but she listened. "Well," said Cree "when we were walking to school the other morning, he called me over and told me about the body odor thing. Told me I should do something about it. I was so ashamed. I could not look at him and asked him what he meant and why he would say that. He just stared at me. Then as I was walking away, he told me I'm too fresh." Hayly froze, she had heard those words before. She cringed. Hayly gently squeezed Cree's hand.

Cree was crying uncontrollably now. Hayly put her arm around her while Cree told her everything that happened. Fighting through a flood of tears, Cree described to Hayly how Uncle Warren came to her home, touched her inappropriately; how she screamed; how she tried to resist; how he covered her mouth with his hand; how he lifted her to her bedroom and threw her on her bed and raped her; how he told her that no one would believe her if she told anyone because she was too fresh. Hayly was shocked and didn't believe her at first. She thought of her uncle who worked hard, who was well-respected in the church, who brought her family lots of fish, fruit, and veggies but... who did snap at her one weekend and called her fresh, and who seemed to have a secret family. How could Cree have known he'd called her fresh too? She couldn't be lying!

Hayly went to Cree's room, opened the door, and looked around, she saw evidence of what Cree said happened and was stunned. It was true! The truth hit her hard, Hayly felt her heart begin to beat faster as she realized that Cree was telling her the truth. Hayly's ears felt hot,

there was a knot in her stomach, she felt sick, angry, scared, and upset. Hayly stood frozen on the spot. What should she do? "We have to tell someone," Hayly insisted. "No! We can't! Nobody will believe me!" Cree cried. Hayly hugged Cree and encouraged her that she had to tell. After what felt like forever, Hayly called Auntie Nina who closed the bookstore and coffee shop and came right over.

They told her the truth. " Cree I am so sorry Warren did this to you. Your mom needs to know and the police too. No one is supposed to touch any of you like that. You're just kids and it's wrong. I believe you." "You do?" Cree asked in a small voice. "Yes, Cree I do because he's done it before," said Auntie Nina Akosua, angrily. Hayly didn't think she could be more shocked, but she was. "He's done it before? Who to? How do you know?" Hayly asked. "Your uncle Warren has two children with a lady who lives up north. She accused him of attacking and raping her when she was a teenager. Nobody believed her, especially the bishop and the church folks but I've always had my suspicions. I've always made sure your mum keeps you busy at the weekends so you're not alone with him." Hayly thought about the weekends, how her parents almost trail Uncle Warren around and insist he stay for a meal. How they have always encouraged Hayly to spend time with Auntie Nina or Cree when Uncle Warren is around. "Are my parents afraid of him?" she asked in a small voice. "Is that why they don't want you there, but they let him come over?" Aunt Nina explains that it's not 'just' because she has a child and isn't married, it's because it helps keep Hayly safe by having her away so Hayly can visit her. "But how will they believe me when they've never believed the mother of his children?" asked Cree. "Ms. Enid," Hayly said.

Hayly called Cree's Mom, Tessa, they tell the police, and Uncle Warren is arrested later that day. Ms. Enid explains everything that she saw and heard at Cree's house to the police, but she hadn't spoken about it because she didn't want to be seen as a busybody.

Now that Uncle Warren was arrested, other children can be safe. It turns out that he had been trying to persuade the mother of his children to see his daughters, but she wouldn't let him as she was afraid, he would harm them too. Thanks to Cree's honesty, and Hayly's bravery they are now safe too.

Hayly enjoys her weekends where she's awoken not by the sound of her uncle's voice, but only by the soft nudging of Cocoa's nose, and the seagulls looking for food by the seashore. Although her friend Cree still has a lot of healing to do and her mom and Hayly's family are still in shock, a great amount of tension seems to have left the Simmons family and the wider Mount Vernon community.

Hayly stemmed the Tide.

-The End-

Resources to report suspected Child Abuse

1-800-422-4453   In the United States and Canada:
1-242-422-2763   In The Bahamas
0808-800-5000   In United Kingdom
1800-55-1800   In Australia

"And you will understand all too soon That you, my children of battle, are your heroes"
-Nikki Giovanni

Nikki Giovanni (1993) "Ego Tripping and Other Poems for Young People," p49, Chicago Review Press

TERMS

- **APPROPRIATE REMARKS**

These are words said by someone that are good and make you feel good.
Examples:
1. You are pretty/handsome
2. I believe you
3. You are loved or I love you
4. Good job.

- **INAPPROPRIATE REMARKS**

These are words said by someone to you either by yourself or in front of others that make you feel uncomfortable or uneasy. Examples:
1. You smell bad,
2. You are ugly.
3. You are an idiot
4. You are too fresh

- **APPROPRIATE OR GOOD TOUCH**

This is an action by someone that makes you feel valued and good. Examples:
1. A hug from a friend,
2. A pat on the back by a trusted adult or friend
3. A handshake
4. A pat on the head

- **INAPPROPRIATE TOUCH**

This is an action by someone that makes you feel uncomfortable or uneasy.
Examples:
1.   Someone touches you after you have asked them not to or said No, that is an inappropriate touch. A trusted adult should be told right away.
2.   Someone touches you in or around your private parts or genitalia with a part of his or her body or an object, this is a bad touch and should be reported to a trusted adult right away.

TRUSTED ADULT
Examples:
1.   Parents
2.   Teachers
3.   Doctor
4.   Police

About the Author

Elizabeth Thompson is a mother of four sons, an advocate, a creative author, and a poet. She was born and raised in the Commonwealth of The Bahamas, studied in Canada, and England after which she was called to English and The Bahamas' Bar in 1994. Elizabeth Thompson practiced law from 1995 to 2014 when she retired as Barrister and Counsel and Attorney at Law in good standing and relocated to the United States. Elizabeth has traveled extensively to countries in South America, Asia, Africa, Europe, the United States, Canada, and the Caribbean. During her career, she represented The Bahamas at numerous conferences and seminars as a speaker in

the field of anti-money laundering and white-collar crime. She has also worked in the financial services sector. However, her most rewarding work has been advocating for the rights of child victims of neglect and abuse.

Elizabeth Thompson is currently a Registered Behavioral Technician, a Florida certified Advocate for the empowerment of survivors of domestic violence and a Florida certified Professional Guardian qualified to act for and on behalf of vulnerable adults.

Elizabeth has provided her website below not only for the purchase of this book but also as a safe space for children or adults to reach out confidentially for support and/or encouragement.

www.akosuamaatcreative.com

Lightning Source UK Ltd.
Milton Keynes UK
UKHW051135260722
406324UK00003B/21

9 798985 452617